TO THE
POINT

bOUNCE

TO THE
POINT

PATRICK JONES

darbycreek

MINNEAPOLIS

Darby Creek
A division of Lerner Publishing Group, Inc.
241 First Avenue North
Minneapolis, MN 55401 USA

For reading levels and more information, look up this title at www.lernerbooks.com.

Front cover: © iStockphoto.com/MistikaS

Main body text set in Janson Text LT Std 12/17.5.
Typeface provided by Adobe Systems.

Library of Congress Cataloging-in-Publication Data

The Cataloging-in-Publication Data for *To the Point* is on file at the Library of Congress.
ISBN 978-1-5124-1124-9 (lib. bdg.)
ISBN 978-1-5124-1208-6 (pbk.)
ISBN 978-1-5124-1135-5 (EB pdf)

LC record available at https://lccn.loc.gov/2015044797

Manufactured in the United States of America
1-39639-21282-3/18/2016

To Megan V, for helping me find my values

TEAM CAPTAIN HANDBOOK
Hueytown High School

The coaches of the Hueytown High School
Gopher athletic teams take the role of team
captain seriously. The title of team captain is
not simply given to the best player on the team,
but rather, the title is earned by the player
who is willing to do the most to help the team
achieve. While it is true that some people are
born with natural athletic ability and leadership
skills, it is also true that these traits will emerge
with hard work, discipline, and patience. A
true leader leads by example and is ALWAYS a
role model.

The following are the characteristics and
qualities of a successful team captain:

1. Intelligence. A captain must be smart on and off the field. An athlete's grades in school are important. We emphasize academics because we know that if you are smart enough to work hard in the classroom, then you will also be intelligent in your athletic endeavors.

2. Loyalty. A coach must have TOTAL trust and faith in the captain's ability to carry out orders as well as encourage others to do the same. The captain is "on point" between the team and the coach, but the point ALWAYS tips toward the side of the coaching staff.

3. Humility. Captains sacrifice their own desires and place the best interest of the team first. A team captain cheers the loudest, but also listens humbly to the coach.

4. Strength. A team captain is mentally and physically tough. A captain is a role model during workouts and practices, ALWAYS pushing on when everyone else wants to quit.

5. Positive attitude. A team needs a captain with a positive attitude to carry them through tough times. A captain is NEVER negative about the coach, teachers, team, or school.

6. Integrity. If a team captain demonstrates these other attributes, then they demonstrate the most important trait: integrity. A captain with integrity is trusted to do the right thing for the greater good, never takes shortcuts, and ALWAYS shows good sportsmanship.

Congratulations on being selected as team captain, and good luck in your upcoming season!

"He's cheating." I stare at Coach Duncan. He's all deer-caught-in-the-sight-of-my-hunting-rifle. He peers at me through thick glasses befitting someone older than thirty.

"Their center is cheating up on a defense," I explain during our last time-out. Even though I'm not starting, as captain, I always join the huddle. Yo starts at point guard and eats most of my minutes, so I'm able to concentrate intensely on the details of the game. "Show can slip in behind him."

"Show" is Ed Showkowski, our six-foot-ten center. "He's right, Coach," Show mumbles.

Why Show didn't point this out himself,

I don't know. Yo, the point guard who should be court general, didn't see it either. You need keen bench eyes like mine to really see the game.

"Dallas, do it," Coach tells Yo. His name is Dallas, but I call him Yo, short for Yo-Yo, because his mood is always up and down.

We're behind by one with fifteen seconds left. This play decides the game. A loss would be our first of the season. I glance up at the stands and see Aunt Angie, smiling but clueless. Above her and the rest of our fans, ten state championship banners hang from the rafters. There are a lot of them, but the most recent one is the same age as me. It's been eighteen years since we won state.

The team runs onto the court, and Connie Harris, the head cheerleader, tries getting the crowd fired up. I think Connie was selected more for her shape than her skills, so I take over.

I stand on the bench rather than sit on it. I thrust my right arm high in the air and shout, "Go!" The crowd responds. I pump my left and shout, "Phers!" They answer the same back and forth, louder and louder until it's a runaway train of support. "Go-phers! Go-phers!"

The clock starts, the ball goes in, and just as I called it, Yo passes to a wide-open Show. Show slams home two, putting us in front. Hoover calls time, and we're back on the bench. I slap backs, pound fists, and hand out compliments like candy at Halloween.

"Randy, I want you in for the final play," Coach says. Yo groans like he's been hacked.

"Don't you think Yo has this?" I ask under my breath. Any question to Coach borders on defiance.

Coach says nothing. He points toward the scorer's table. My feet hit the court at the same time as Yo's backside rests on the bench. "We own them," I tell my fantastic four teammates.

I fail at swatting down the inbound pass but sprint back on D. I'm on point, like I am when I go hunting with Show, Show's dad, and Yo, like Mom used to be in our house, and like I am from the bench. The Hoover point guard dribbles like he's scared of the ball. I trash-talk just loud enough for only his rabbit ears to hear.

The guard passes then cuts toward the basket, but I'm a fly on this turd. He won't touch the ball again. The ball goes around and around, but not toward the net. With one second left, their forward forces a jumper from the baseline that clangs off the rim in unison with the buzzer.

I sprint toward the center of the court and my team meets me there. My right arm shoots up, "Go!" My left arm follows with a fist, "Phers!" The crowd roars louder than an Alabama thunderstorm. "Go-phers! Go-phers!" Everybody on the team yells along, except for Yo.

Connie bounces toward us, to my delight, with her squad behind her. I'm envious of their view. She joins in on the cheers that are growing stronger. Everybody but Yo leaves the bench, including Coach. We're jumping and cheering in sync like a mean machine.

"Hey, Randy!" a voice says.

I turn. It's Prof, known to others as

Lance. He hands me the ball. "O Captain! my Captain!" Prof pats me on the back. I shrug, confused. "Walt Whitman," Prof says.

"Walt who?" I think he's a writer of some kind, but me and books are mortal enemies.

"Never mind." Prof says stuff like this, which is why I call him Prof, short for professor. His college scholarship hopes, unlike those of most of the team, ride on his genius, not his game.

I try talking to Connie, but she's in Yo's eyes, ears, and throat. Standing at center court, surrounded by my team and showered with cheers, I've never felt prouder. I wave to Aunt Angie, who waves back. I'd wave to Mom, but she's in the hospital. She'd be proud too, I know. That's she safe, I can only hope.

I glare at my returned history test like it's an enemy, not an academic assessment.

Another C on an exam and I will lose the captain's C on my basketball uniform.

C to shining C.

In B-ball, I get an E for ability and an A for effort. I only C action when coach needs D. D also stands for dyslexia, which I have, and dumb, like I feel. My life's a mixed-up alphabet soup.

"How'd you do?" Prof asks. He should be in AP classes, but I think it would embarrass him. I don't bother to ask him about the A on his test or the smile on his face that he can't hide.

I cock my hand like a pistol and jam a finger in my mouth. He laughs, but I don't. I turn to catch Yo and Show's expressions since they are worse students than me. I expect to see frowns, but instead I see smiles. I'm confused by that—maybe as much as our teacher, Mrs. Russo.

After she hands back the test, she stops by my desk. "Randy, see me after class."

Mrs. Russo goes over the test, and each time she reviews one of my wrong answers, I wince.

"Dallas, share your answer to number four about Pickett's Charge," Mrs. Russo says.

Yo starts, stops, and stumbles over his words. Show's laughing, and so are Connie and Reg.

"That's enough." Mrs. Russo tries sounding tough.

"Help Yo out," I hard-whisper to Prof. He jumps in like he was chasing a loose ball.

There's sighing when Prof talks, especially from Yo, Show, and Connie. The rest of class goes on like normal: Russo flapping her lips, lots of faces resting on gray desks, and me trying to stay awake, take notes, and pay attention. I succeed at just the first.

Once the bell rings, I drag myself to the front of the room. Russo sits at her desk.

"Randy, is everything okay? Your grades have—" She stops herself from grinding salt in my wounds.

"I'm just busy with basketball," I remind her. I don't tell her the other half of the truth, about Mom, nor do I tell her about all the extra responsibilities I have as team captain. "I'm okay."

"You know the school has a tutoring program." She might know history, but not the present. There are two tutoring programs: one for the basketball team that Coach has a college kid from Samford run, and another run by NHS for everybody else. "If that would help, then—"

"I don't have time." Tutoring happens before school, and I can't sacrifice any sleep.

She glances at her computer and taps on the keyboard. Her face sours as if she swallowed a lemon when she inspects the screen. "It's not just my class, is it?"

Students shuffle in for the next hour, so I mumble a non-answer and escape toward biology, another class I'm failing. There's no doubt I'll hear the same shaming speech there from Miss Sanders.

In the hallway, Yo and Show lean against the wall, laughing too loudly for this early in the morning.

"What's so funny, guys?" They glance at each other, but not at me. "So how'd you do?"

They flash their A test papers in my eyes like a blinding flashlight. They *never* get A's. I started the second half of last season because Yo lost his eligibility from having failing grades.

"Maybe I should study with you guys," I say. "That would set a good example."

"Or study with Mr. Smith," Yo says. That's Coach's tutor. I tell them the same thing I told Russo about not having time. They know some of the stuff about my mom, but not the worst of it.

"A few cheerleaders are there too, Captain," Show adds.

My face turns redder than my hair. "In that case, I'll charge ahead like I was Pickett."

"Who is Pickett?" Yo asks, surprised. He holds his test in his left hand where question four asked about Pickett's Charge. It was a question he got right. I suspect something's wrong.

I glance down at the sparkling clean kitchen table in Aunt Angie's house. Compared to the house that I left to move in with Angie, any clear flat surface looks spotless and sterile. Mom never seemed to be able to hang onto her jobs, but for all the time she spent at home, she was mostly in bed.

"How was practice, Randy?" She offers me bottled water, but I reach for a Red Bull.

"Long and hard," I explain, "but longer and harder for me than everyone else." I remind her of all the duties I have as captain. I meet with Coach before and after practice. I run warm-up exercises. Coach also has me helping struggling players and underclassmen improve their game.

"It's a full-time job," Angie says and smiles. Her face reminds me of Mom, except for the smile. Even Mom's half smiles didn't last long. "You need to slow down or . . ." Angie sips from her before-dinner cocktail instead of finishing her sentence.

"I need to study." I chug down the Red Bull. She shakes her head in disapproval. I assume she disapproves of the energy drink rather than my improvement plan. "I have an algebra test tomorrow."

"Can I help?" Angie is a librarian. Aside from the Dewey decimal system, she knows less about math than anyone, except maybe Yo, Show, and Connie. Math has been my one okay subject because numbers, unlike letters, I can read. Numbers stand straight like loyal soldiers.

I don't answer and instead I play question give-and-go with my aunt. "How is Mom?"

A sip from her drink serves as her answer about something we usually avoid discussing

because it just hurts too much. I snatch another
Red Bull, tuck it under my arm, and take the
full plate of home-cooked grilled chicken with
all the sides. I head into my room, which is
Angie's old office. I sit down on the hard chair
surrounded by book-filled shelves. The words
in them shame and mock me.

I take four sips, three bites, and yawn twice.
I try hard to keep my eyes open, but I sense
that I'm failing. It makes me think of Mom
trying to stay out of the hospital but being too
weak, and I'm not strong enough for both of
us. I can't captain our team of two if Mom's too
hurt to fulfill her role: being my mom.

"Randy, wake up." Miss Torrez pokes the arm cradling my head. I focus on her wide mouth as she points at the floor where my test lies like a wounded warrior. I pick it up.

My eyes must look like red saucers to Miss Torrez. I was awake on and off all night last night, thinking bad thoughts about Mom and happy thoughts about Connie.

"You won't have time to finish the test," Torrez says through my haze.

I check the clock. Ten minutes to finish ten math problems. It'd be like standing at the other end of the court with my back to the basket and hitting a jumper. "Why didn't you wake—"

"I'm your teacher, not an alarm clock," she says. I hear Yo and Show laugh too loudly. I turn to evil-eye them and see that they're on their phones with no tests in front of them.

Panic slices through me. The pencil's hard to hold with a trembling hand. "Could I—" I say to Miss Torrez as she walks away.

"Do you want to see my answers?" I hear Prof whisper. I shake my head. I will not cheat, and he should know better than to tempt me with that juicy but worm-filled apple. I bear down.

"Shut up!" I shout at Prof, at the ticking clock, and at Coach's voice stuck in my head. The only thing louder than my words is the ringing bell. The only things whiter than my face are the blank spaces on the test. Connie joins Yo at the door and my heart breaks a little bit more. I'm a decaying zombie and every day a little bit more of me falls off.

I rise to leave and catch up with Show. "Number one sure was hard. What did you get?"

Show keeps walking, not answering. He heads in one direction, I go in the other. I think about asking Torrez to retake the test, but she's an athlete hater. I'm not sure how half the seniors on my team got into her class. I'll ask Coach. He solves problems. Although I heard a rumor that if he doesn't win state this year, he'll lose his job. Maybe that's a problem his captain can solve for him.

"Play your game like any other game," I tell Yo
and Show. "It's about the team." But I wonder if
they can hear me through their big heads and
burning ears. The school buzzed all day because
they got featured in an al.com story about top
Birmingham area high school prospects.

They nod like they agree, but I sense
they're playing me. "Sure thing, *Cap-tain*,"
Yo says. He nods again in agreement, but the
smirk on his face sends a disrespectful message
my way.

Show nods in agreement too, and the
three of us make our way from the gym to
the team bus. They head toward the back,

but I sit up front next to Coach. I start to tell him about Yo's attitude, but Coach shuts me down. "Integrity, Randy. Nobody likes or respects a snitch."

My mind flashes not to Yo or Show, but to Angie. I imagine the look on her face when she made the call about Mom.

"You might want to review the traits of a successful captain again."

"I'm worried about the team. I heard that you might lose your job if—"

"What happens to me doesn't matter." I don't believe Coach, just like I don't believe Yo. I guess after so many years of Mom saying "I'm okay, Randall," I've learned to sense when someone is lying to me.

"We can't win if they start freelancing and not running your plays," I say.

Coach taps his phone a few times. He puts it in my face. On it is a school document with my name on top and my letter grades below, all of them falling down. "You need to attend Mr. Smith's tutoring class starting tomorrow." It's not the tone of a suggestion, but of an order.

"Whatever you want me to do, Coach," I say, showing my loyalty through those seven words.

"Always." Coach bears the same smirk on his face that Yo had earlier.

The rest of the bus ride, I bury my face in my history book while Coach texts. I try to sleep but his constant tapping and scrolling makes that impossible. I follow his lead and text Aunt Angie to ask her to buy more Red Bull. I'll need fuel to fire my brain at zero hour tutoring time.

I oversleep by ten minutes, so I miss the first
bus. I take off running in the cold morning
rain, giving my legs the workout they didn't
get last night. Coach let Yo play almost
the entire game. He subbed for him with a
freshman rather than me. I guess my minutes
on the court depend on my attendance at
Smith's zero hour tutoring. In Coach's math,
loyalty equals obedience.

It's not just the lost sleep that's making
me dread tutoring. It's also the memories
it will bring back from elementary school,
when I was in the remedial classes. I was
always getting special help. Like a bad

nightmare, I remember struggling over every letter, word, sentence, paragraph, and page. It's no wonder that I run all the hurdle races during track season.

Somebody must have seen me walk through the door, because I hear laughter as I enter the room. Who can laugh this early in the morning? It's Yo and Connie. They're looking at something on Yo's phone. They're not the only ones. Everybody's looking down at their phones rather than up on the chalkboard, which is totally empty.

"You Sullivan?" the young guy perched on the edge of the teacher's desk asks me. I nod.

"Have a seat." He points to the worst one in the room, in the back, far away from Connie. She's with Yo front and center, as always. I do as I'm told, as always. "Coach says you're team captain." Another nod. He must think I've got no brain in my head or muscles in my neck.

"Well, that doesn't matter to me." He sits down next to me. He smells like the jasmine tea that Mom used to drink in the morning.

"What matters is that you do the work."

I look around the room. Nobody is working, but I don't say anything. "Rule one is you listen to me. Rule two is you keep your mouth shut. That's it. Two rules. You understand?"

"Yes," I say to prove I'm not mute or dumb, no matter what my grades say.

"I have a list of your classes, your teachers, your current grades, and your upcoming tests." He thrusts his phone at me. "Is everything here right?" I yawn as an answer.

"You have a vocabulary test in biology class next week," Mr. Smith drones.

"I was doing good in that class, but . . ." I never finish any sentence where the last true words are *then my mom went into the hospital.* Instead I say, "But stuff happened."

"Stuff is always going to happen, Mr. Sullivan. That's why Coach hired me to help all of you." I'm not sure how Yo and Connie rapping along to a video is helping anybody, but I don't ask. I want to show him I can keep my mouth shut. "You got your biology book with you?"

I pull out the book and open it up. He seems disinterested. "Is this your email?"

I glance at his phone again. It's my personal email address, not my school email. We're always told that all school stuff, even when it's from Coach, must go through the school email.

"That's it," I say.

"I'll send you something that will help you."

"I need it."

He starts to say something, but we're distracted by Yo's two-left-feet dance moves. He's graceful and serious on the court, but the opposite off it. I wish I could cut loose like Yo, but as captain, I have to play the role of leader 24/7. No wonder I can't sleep.

"You think they're gonna make it to the pros?" Mr. Smith points at Yo and Show.

"Only if they play the game the right way." I try to hide the disdain that's in my voice because neither of them listened to me the other night. We won—in fact, by our biggest margin all year—except Show and Yo hogged the ball. The two of them scored half the points. That's not a team.

"That's the important thing, Mr. Sullivan." Smith stands up and readjusts his worn red and blue Samford University Bulldogs sweatshirt, an odd clothing choice given the fancy watch he's wearing. "Playing the game the right way. You do what I tell you and your grades will go up."

"You must be some tutor," I remark.

For the first time this morning, Mr. Smith laughs almost louder than Yo.

"Let's work!" I shout at the top of my lungs and clap even louder. "It is Carver time!"

Our game tomorrow night is against crosstown rival Carver High. They beat us twice last year: once in the regular season and again in the first round of the state tourney. Like us, they're undefeated so far, but unlike us, they play the game the right way: a team of five, not two. Everybody works hard doing warm-up exercises, except Yo and Show, who dog it. And Prof.

I shout more encouragement from the front, but then I walk over to Prof. "You okay?"

He doesn't say anything, all steely-eyed and

silent. Very non-Prof. "Prof, talk to me." I pull his left arm gently, and we walk toward the side of the gym. "You had a good game."

Prof sniffs. Since he backs up Show, his last game consisted of less than six minutes. "He's a big guy, he's gonna tire out," I say. "Stay positive. Keep your game sharp. You'll get your time."

"Thanks, Captain," These are two words I never tire of hearing from a teammate. "You need me to tutor you?" I don't answer, but instead I shout at the team to work hard. He asks again.

"No, we have this—" Then I stop. *Rule two is you keep your mouth shut.* I know why: because Smith's tutoring is worthless. His help for the bio test was to send me a word definition list, but just twenty words out of the possible hundred that might be on the test. They were in some weird random order. Add in the past two mornings of just him and me in the room, and tutoring is a bust. "I'm good."

"O Captain! my Captain!" Prof laughs. I join in but I still don't get it, so I ask.

"It's from a poem Walt Whitman wrote about President Lincoln after he was killed."

I smack Prof on the back. "Lucky for me that high school team captains are rarely assassinated." The smile on my face vanishes when I hear Yo and Show acting like losers.

Prof thanks me again, and as I walk back toward the front of the team, I'm weighing options. Yo and Show laugh again, and I know I have my own civil war to fight.

Two days later, I walk into bio class to a chorus of "Congrats, Randy, big win!" They don't know the half of it. We were down ten against Carver going into the fourth quarter when Coach rested Yo, mainly to keep him from fouling out. I came in and distributed the ball—unlike Velcro Yo—and spread out the defense. Then Show, maybe angry he wasn't getting the ball off rebounds since good shots were going in and he wasn't getting tips, pressed too hard for the ball. Prof replaced Show when he fouled out. With seconds left, I laser-beamed a pass to Prof, who faked the shot, hurled it back to the point where I was wide open, and I hit the game-winning jumper from the top of the key.

"Mr. Sullivan, very good job indeed, but now onto something important," bio teacher Miss Sanders says as she hands us the test. "Twenty questions, twenty minutes. Turn it over and go."

For some reason, her super strict tone cracks up Connie. Yo and Show might have laughed too, but oddly, they're not here. The flapping of flipping papers fails to distract me from Connie. The back of her head is beautiful. If only she hadn't rejected me to my face every time I feebly attempted to flirt. Before she and Yo were together, I made more bad passes at Connie than I ever made on the court.

"I'm cold," Connie says. She pulls her hoodie over her head. Just before she does, I notice her slip a bud into her ear with her right hand. A hand that then slips into her jeans pocket.

That's not even the strangest thing. The weirdest thing is that the twenty words Sanders wants us to define are the same twenty terms in the exact same order as the words in the file Mr. Smith emailed me. He is either so lucky he should play the lottery, or like a foul-prone player, he's a hacker.

We're a few minutes into what is now the easiest test I've ever taken, when Yo and Show enter the room. Sanders beats them down with a frown but then hands them the test. They make their way to a table in the back, giggling like middle school girls. As they pass by, I notice just peeking out of Yo's back pocket is Sanders's test, but with the answers already filled out.

9

Practicing after a win is harder, but my heart isn't in it. How can I throw around a twenty-two ounce ball when I've got this weight on my shoulders? Show and Yo give me the silent treatment after practice. I wonder if it's because Prof and I took their hero status in the last game or if it's a message to me: keep your mouth shut for the good of the team. That's what captains do—what is good for the team. But as I walk to the bus stop, I wonder how something so wrong could ever be good.

I'm lost in a raucous jungle of jumbling thoughts when my phone buzzes. Aunt Angie.

"Randy, your mom wants to see you." It's taken

three weeks for her to say the words I've wanted to hear ever since Mom went into the hospital again. "Stay at school. I'll pick you up." The weight on my shoulders just doubled, and I can't move.

"Randy, great game," Connie whispers. I didn't hear her walk up behind me, but now she's almost in my ear. I inhale the scent of lip gloss, gum, and perfume. I've got sweet odor overload.

Words get tangled in my throat like letters do on the page until I mumble, "Thanks."

"We should get together sometime." More whispers, like it's a secret. What about Yo? "I mean, we both are working for the same thing, encouraging the team to win. You busy now?"

"Anytime but now, and I'd love to." She motions for my phone. I hand it over like she is a thief pointing a pistol in my face. Connie punches in her digits then hands it back. "Don't make me wait too long. I don't like guys I can't trust to follow through, know what I mean?"

I'm speechless again. She puts up her hoodie and walks toward her Lexus. My body's still reacting to all of that when Angie pulls up in her old Honda. "Get in, Randy."

I open the door, toss my bag at my feet,
climb in, and snap the seat belt. I'm safe. Right.

"Is something wrong?" I ask.

"She just wants to see *you*, that's all I know.
You'll only have a few minutes."

I press Angie for more information, but she
turns on NPR so she can learn about problems
in Africa, problems with waterfowl, and other
stuff instead of everything I've got on my plate.
I can't carry these burdens by myself. By the
time we get to the UAB Hospital, I'm wallowing
in a salty sea of self-pity. I suck it up, pull in my
tears, and walk with Angie into the hospital. I
know the drill. I travel light with only my ID—
everything else stays in the Honda. The guard
looks me over and makes a call before he opens
the door. For a second, when it opens, the words
on the door—Psychiatric Ward—vanish.

Maybe because she's so troubled and tortured
herself, Mom knows something's bothering me.
I try to talk about her recovery and when she's
coming home, but she's not having it. "What is
it, Randall?"

So I tell her about Mr. Smith. She squints

her green eyes at me. They won't let her wear her glasses. I tell her that I don't know what to do. "I don't want to be a snitch."

"Like my sister." Mom packs thirty pounds of anger into just three words. She runs her left hand over her shaved head. Her skull spurts thousands of tiny red hairs like the freckles on her face.

"What do I do, Mom?"

She licks her dry lips. "Randy, you need to follow your values."

The burden becomes a baseball bat so I swing with fury. "You mean like *you*."

I wait for sad tears or angry shouts. Mom rarely has in-betweens. "Yes," Mom says.

"You left me," I whisper, because that's what you do with a secret.

"I did that, Randall, because I followed *my* values. Protecting you was more important to me than anything else."

"Protecting me from what?" I avoid looking at the still-healing scar on her wrist.

"From me, Randy, from me." Her words are sharper than the bloody razor blade I found next to the bathtub.

10

"So that's what I think, Coach." I stare at my white Nikes because I can't bear his brown eyes bearing down on me as I describe to him how Mr. Smith's tutoring was just cheating.

"What did I tell you before, Randy?" His voice is harsh. "Nobody likes a snitch."

"But it's wrong." He barely reacted while I was telling him, which means he already knew. Maybe it was even his idea.

"Who else have you told?"

I never noticed how tattered my shoes were before. "Nobody but you."

His chair squeaks. I sneak a peek and he's reclining, arms behind his head like somebody who just finished a big meal. "That's good. That's the right thing to do. We are family and things like this stay in a family." His tone almost implies he knows more about Mom than I thought. But how could he?

"What are you going to do about it?" I ask Coach.

"I'll look into it. What are *you* going to do?" he asks, as if he were playing a trump card.

I can tell from his tone and posture that there's only one right answer. "Just tell you, that's it."

Coach reaches into his desk, pulls out some papers, and pushes them toward me. It's the captain's handbook. He hands me a yellow highlighter. "Maybe you need to study this again."

I nod in agreement and then take the papers. They feel so heavy. "Thanks, Coach."

He doesn't say good-bye, which is fine because Yo and Show are standing in front of my locker as if they're the locker room welcoming committee. From the hard looks on their faces, they're not happy to see me.

"Don't mess this up for me, Randy!" Yo shouts. "We shouldn't have let you in on it."

Show says nothing, but instead puts his paws under my pits and lifts me like a dumbbell.

"The only path for me getting out of this pit is a scholarship." Yo spits every "p" in my face. "Don't blow this for me. You're the captain, so be the captain. Sacrifice for the good of the team."

Show adds the exclamation point by bouncing my head against the locker, and he then drops me like a bad habit.

I start the "Go-pher" chant even though
we're ahead by fifteen at the half and playing
on the road. Coach gave a fired-up locker-
room speech, but he didn't give me a chance
to say my part. Just like I hadn't touched the
ball all game. Coach won't even look at me,
which tells me that the only contact I should
expect during the second half is my butt
against the bench.

Not that my team needs me. Yo and Show
pick apart the Pelham defense with ease.

When we're ahead by twenty-five in the
fourth, Coach pulls Show and puts Prof in
his place. Show wipes the sweat off his shaved

head and throws the towel to me. "Great game, Show!" I shout.

"Save it, Randy."

"No, really, your game keeps getting better," I say, but he's head-down, breathing heavy. I tap him on the shoulder. "I bet you have scouts up in the stands breathing heavier than you."

Show crosses his arms, leans back on the bench, and watches the game, looking bored. After Yo hits a jumper, which isn't his job, Coach decides to pull him. I stand. He calls for Fresh, which is what everybody calls Stevie Richards, the only freshman on the team. As long as I'm standing, I give Fresh a brief pep talk as he walks by. "Thanks, Captain," he says.

"Great game, Yo," I start, but Yo walks by me as if I don't exist and heads toward the end of the bench like he's not part of the team. Like he's better than us. He's better than Fresh, who turns over the ball on his first trip down the court, and his second. On his third try, he walks.

"Yo, back in!" Yo moves from the bench to the court like he has molasses shoes.

As soon as Fresh comes off the court, I wrap an arm around him and walk with him toward the end of the bench. "It's one game. Don't worry about it, Fresh. Shake it off."

Fresh shakes his head like he doesn't believe me. "I blew my one chance."

I look past Fresh toward Coach and wonder if I blew my one chance to do the right thing.

The email from Mr. Smith comes two days before Mr. Rios' Spanish test. It's not a list of words to study, but the test itself. A sound file is attached. I open it and listen. It's Smith reading the answers. My finger hovers over the delete key. I get close to pressing it, but then I think about how much I needed help. *There's no I in team*, I think, *but there is an I in the word* integrity. I delete the files.

Sure enough, when the test comes back the next morning, there is a D on it. D as in defeated, distracted, and discouraged. The high fives from Connie, Yo, and Show tell me everything I need to know. If Coach looked into the tutoring program, he did so only to see that it would continue. I won't show up again at zero hour since Mr. Smith has zero benefit for me.

When the period ends, I drag myself toward the gym rather than the cafeteria. I'll run drills with Fresh and Prof so they can regain their confidence. Maybe someone can help me with mine, but instead Yo stops me and rubs my face in it. He pushes his A test under my chin.

"How'd you do, Captain?" He's seriously got that silly middle school girl giggle down.

"Look, you play your game and I'll play mine, and we'll see how it comes out."

"If you don't get with the program, you won't even be on my team." *My team?*

I grab Yo's shoulders and pull him closer. "Yo, it's cheating. It's just not fair."

He knocks my hand off his shoulders and gets in my face. His mouth hangs open. His jagged teeth look like little white mountains. "Unfair? Unfair is living in twenty houses the first sixteen years of your life. Unfair is not having a mom you can count on or a dad who even cares if you exist. Unfair is growing up going to bad schools with bad teachers surrounded by bad kids in a bad neighborhood, yet my grandmother expects me to be good. That's unfair."

"Look, I don't want to—"

"If it's gonna be unfair, it's time it's in my favor!" He bangs his chest and walks away.

Show tumbles to the court clutching his side
but twisting his ankle as he falls. Everybody on
the team looks concerned, except me because
I'm busy glaring at the Lee High player—
number 47—who elbowed Show in the ribs. It
was a blow that felled Show like a sick tree.

Coach and I run out onto the court: Coach
to check out Show, me to put 47 on notice.
"You try that crap again and I'll take you out,"
I threaten the much bigger player. He laughs
at me.

Coach and I help Show to his feet, but he
can't place any weight on his left ankle so we
help him hop off the court. When we get to

the bench, we ease him down. Coach checks on Show's pain. I turn toward Prof. "It's on you, Prof." Together we stare at the scoreboard above to see the uncommon sight: the Hueytown home side with fewer points than the visiting team.

Prof goes in and plays strong defense, but 47 manhandles him. The refs let it go. Even though it goes against the captain's code of sportsmanship, I yell at the refs to make the call. With Show out, the pressure falls upon Yo. He tries to do too much. He shoots when he should pass. He takes chances on defense instead of playing it safe. When Yo commits his final foul—on 47, no less—it sends him to the showers, 47 to the line, and me into the game. Maybe Fresh was right, he blew his one chance. Coach might want to punish me, but he wants to win more.

I run onto the court, but rather than heading for my position, I get in the face of 47 at the line. "You're going to miss these two, and then we're going to win this game."

He laughs again. But he's not laughing

when he misses the first and then the second foul shot. Prof gathers the rebound and moves it down court. I glance at the score. A quick pass, a cut, a pick, and we crawl back. I put pressure on D, force a turnover, and pass to Reg, our shooting forward. Another two. And another. And another. Their coach calls time out. We head to our bench.

Coach gives us a pep talk, while Connie tries getting the crowd into it. I do my "Go-pher" bit as I walk back onto the court. We've got one minute to get three points. They inbound and pass to 47, who barrels hard into Prof. Prof stands his ground, so it's a charge. We get the ball back and, even with the clock pressing, I calmly bring the ball up court. I make a quick pass and then sprint for the basket. Prof screens out 47. The ball comes back to the point, and then I put it through the net. One down with forty left. Everybody on our bench stands, even Show. His big mitts slam together, our fans stomp their feet, Connie leads the cheers. The gym feels like it is shaking.

They rush the ball up court. Their point guard looks for a pass. He looks everywhere but at me, so I dive, knock the ball from his hands, and scramble for it. From my knees, I throw it cross-court to Reg, who finds Prof under the basket. Up, in, and we're ahead by one.

I don't steal again, so they work the ball to the basket. Number 47 pushes off Prof, not with a hand to the chest but with a palm to his face. The ref can't ignore it and 47 fouls out. The crowd boos and 47 wipes his eyes like he's crying. Prof's good from the line, so I know he will sink them and put us up by three. It's decision time. I weigh the captain duties as team leader against that of being a role model for sportsmanship.

I decide to sacrifice my body for the good of the team. I chase after 47. "I warned you, Hack!" I yell. He turns, pushes me, but I don't fall. I man up and smack him with stinging fists to his face. Coach and a ref pull me off. The other ref blows his whistle and calls the technical.

As I head to the locker room, I grasp onto Fresh's jersey since he's subbing for me. "I can't do this," Fresh says. I hear the fear of failure in his voice, so I need him to man up.

"You *can* and *will* do this," I say, each word clipped. He runs, inspired, onto the court. I head to the locker room to join Yo, but he's gone. I hear boos from the gym. It means they sank the two fouls shots. Seconds later, I hear a buzzer and cheers. It means we won the game.

"Close the door." Coach points me into the hot seat, or maybe it is the electric chair. Is he going to execute my captaincy? "You're suspended for two games for fighting."

I don't argue. I stare at my shoes, waiting for the other one to drop.

"That's one according to the school and one according to the athletic association, but if it were up to me, I wouldn't make you sit a minute, because you stood up for a teammate."

"Really?" I look down at my knuckles, scuffed from when 47 blocked my punches with his face.

"That's what a captain does, Randy," Coach

says. "He brings fire to the team. He rallies them when they are down. But most of all, he is like a dog protecting his yard and his court."

I've never been called a dog as a compliment before, but I'll take it. "Thanks, Coach."

"You might want to save that thank you, because you're not off the hook just yet." He sounds all stern but I can tell that he's forcing back a smile. "You need to do something for me."

"Anything," I blurt, so happy that the C will stay sewed on my uniform.

"I want you to give a talk to the rest of the team about real sportsmanship. Not the stuff you learned in middle school, but how it works in the real world. Know what I mean?"

"I'm not sure that—"

"In middle school, the world was black and white, but here, it is full of grays. Something might seem wrong at the time, but when you look at the big picture, often it is the right thing to do. Like what you did last night, it was wrong by the rules but the right thing to do. You understand?"

I look over his shoulder at the photos of all his other teams. In each, one player, not always the best, stands next to Coach with a smile on his face and a C on his jersey. "I think so."

"But if you can't tell the difference, then maybe the team needs a new captain."

The words smack against me like my fist against 47's nose. "No, Coach, I got this."

Show's ankle heals well enough for him to practice, but he's not in a good mood, and neither is Yo. Show seems angry, but Yo's withdrawn, sulking, and not his sometimes-smiling self.

After exercises, which Show skips, and shootaround, which Yo tanks, I gather the team together. Coach excuses himself, saying there's something we need to discuss as a team.

I start my speech on sportsmanship, written without help from Mr. Smith or Wikipedia. I get two minutes into it when Fresh, of all people, interrupts. "How is punching a guy in the face good sportsmanship?" He gets grunts of agreement from all except Mr. Smith's group.

"Maybe it broke the rules, but there was a larger point to be made," I explain. "You can't push this team around, and as your captain, it is my job to stand and—"

"We don't need your rah-rah Captain America crap," Show says. "I can stand up for myself." *So says the guy I helped lift up*, I think, *after he fell flat on the hardwood floor.* I wait for Prof to jump to my defense since he's the real guy I stood up for, but he's avoiding my gaze.

"What we need is to play as a team, not for our individual statistics," I say.

"That's because you don't have any stats," Yo says. He stands apart, bouncing a ball.

"What we need," Show fires back at Yo, "is someone who can get me the ball down low, instead of taking jumpers up high." Yo says nothing in return. Soon, it seems everybody but Prof wants to throw in their two points, and no one is listening to me.

Yo takes a ball and hurls it across the gym. It bangs off the backboard, which gets everybody's attention. The silence lasts long enough for him to say, "I think we need a new captain."

I stare at Yo, but he's not backing down. He puffs out his chest like he's some big man. "You want this job, you can have it," I tell Yo through gritted teeth. "Except I don't think you have the right stuff—or the grades."

"I'm getting A's, unlike you." Yo laughs like somebody flipped on his joy switch.

"I wonder why," I snap. The gym goes graveyard silent. Even people not part of Mr. Smith's no-tutor, all-cheat program, like Prof and Fresh, shut their mouths. Everybody knows but nobody talks, so everybody stays clean even as we march through the mud together.

"Look, everybody just lay off—" Prof starts to say. Show shouts him down.

"Nobody cares what you think, bench boy!" Show's voice booms like thunder.

"You got something to say, *Cap-tain*?" Yo exaggerates the last word, almost daring me.

I pause, ball up my fists, and think not about Coach or Yo, but about what Mom said about following my values. The answer emerges easily: "A captain does what is best for his team."

"An undefeated team," Show says.

"A state championship team!" I shout even though I'm ashamed of my silent actions. "We are the champions!" Pretty soon, the team's louder than before, but instead of shouting at each other, they're shouting out those words. "Running with the ball, let's go, Go-phers, let's go!"

Everybody rises from the bench, grabs a ball, and runs foul line to foul line, while I walk to Coach's office to report on the meeting. I knock on the door. He's not alone. It's Mr. Smith.

Smith says nothing. He just nods at me and stands. Before Smith turns to leave, he sets something on Coach's desk. It's a thumb drive, no doubt holding the keys to the grade kingdom.

"So you're captain of the team, Randy, but are you part of the team?" Coach asks.

The real question, I think, is: am I a leader or a follower?

"You can't be captain if you're not eligible,"

Coach says. "You need help with your grades. If you want to stay on this team, then—"

He stops speaking. He puts a pencil in his mouth and chews it. I think about how I used to beg my mom, when she'd go for days without getting out of bed or eating, to get help and how she always said she didn't need help. Mom said she could do things on her own. Like trying to take her own life.

Coach takes the pencil from his mouth. He uses it to push the thumb drive closer. "So?"

"Is there something you want to tell me, Randy?" Mr. Robinson, my school counselor, asks me. It is the first time we've spoken since the start of the school year. It seems that in a school this big, if you're not college or prison bound, people like Robinson don't have time for you.

I finger the thumb drive in my pocket, where it has stayed since practice yesterday. He starts asking more questions, doing a pretty good job of impersonating someone who really cares, and ending with, "I've received early alerts from several of your teachers. You have a D in Spanish?"

"Sí, señor." He doesn't laugh. "I'm distracted by basketball. I don't have time to study."

Robinson frowns. "That's why your coach set up a tutoring program. Have you gone?"

I nod at his cluelessness—or is he trying to see if I'll talk? Does everybody in school know and there's a conspiracy of silence? What's good for the team is anything that helps it to win.

"What are you going to do to get your grades up? Your grade point average is close to making you ineligible for basketball, and I know you don't want that. What is your plan, Randy?"

The green walls of his office resemble puke, which fits, as that's how I feel. "I know other players have improved," Robinson continues. "Is there anything about that tutoring program I should know?"

I mumble two letters: "No." I think about how *loyalty* and *lying* share more than just two letters.

He asks more clueless questions and gives more useless suggestions before excusing me to let in another student he can't help. As I walk to my locker, the thumb drive feels not like a weight in my pocket, but like a stone in my shoe. I limp along until I see Connie standing by my locker. I light up.

"We never got together," I say as I reach for my locker.

She places her hand on mine. She leans close. "You kept your mouth shut?" she whispers. I nod. "You know what happens to closed lips?" Before I can respond, she answers by pressing her lips near mine. I inhale every scent.

I step back. "What about Yo?" She leans in again and doesn't answer. Her mouth is otherwise occupied.

After I get dressed for the last practice of the
regular season, I join the starting five near the
foul line. "About the other day, about everything.
I'm sorry. I want to do the right thing."

"And what's that?" Show asks. I answer by
mock zipping my lips. Yo says nothing.

"The right thing is blowing out Bessemer
tomorrow night and completing our
undefeated season." Everybody cheers in
agreement. I lead the team through warm-up.
The scrimmage game is harder than the real
one might be. I even get the best of Yo. His
feet are in the game, but I can tell his head
is elsewhere. After scrimmage, I lead a loud

"Go-phers!" chant into the locker room.

After showering and getting dressed, the team walks into the gym to find tables filled with pizza and cheerleaders acting as servers. Connie calls me over.

I walk toward her, but I stop when I see Yo headed not for the table, but for the door. "Yo!"

He doesn't turn around. I watch his back as he leaves and feel bad for having stabbed him there. I sprint away from the group and catch up before he exits. "Look, Yo, about Connie."

"It doesn't matter," Yo mumbles. "Nothing matters." He opens the door, and something clicks in my head. I've heard those words before, not from Yo, but from Mom. I head toward Connie.

"Connie, about Yo, I feel bad about—"

"Yo was fun for a while, but then he got so *boring*. He wouldn't do *anything*. I dumped him. Don't you worry." Connie hands me a slice of pizza. "My folks aren't home tonight. You want to come over and study?"

"Study?" I try not to laugh at the idea of it. We both know that studying isn't necessary.

"Well, I'm sure we can find *something* to do together with the time." I pinch myself since I'm in this dream world of captaining an undefeated team and about to hook up with Connie. All it took wasn't hard work or sacrifice, but not living out any of the values I thought I held.

It was a simple transaction: my integrity for my happiness, all sales final.

We can hear Yo's knee pop from the bench.
It is louder than any rifle we ever fired when
Show's dad took the three of us hunting. Yo
crumples in pain, clutching his knee and
screaming in agony. Coach and I race from the
bench, just like we did when Show went down
in the game against Lee High. The other
members of the fantastic four surround Yo on
the court. "My leg, my leg," he repeats. I know
it's not just his leg. It's his game, his season,
and—given we're only five minutes into the
game—it is my final chance to shine.

   We try to get Yo to stand up, but he falls
right back down. The trainer, along with

Fresh and Prof, help him back to the locker room. Nobody moves a muscle among the assembled parents from Bessemer City and Hueytown High.

"You know the game plan, Randy. Stick to it," Coach says as I run out onto the court. I do as I'm told and run the plays with the orange ball, just as Coach had written them on the chalkboard. By the half, Bessemer should be waving a white flag of surrender. I start the second half strong, but scrimmage shape and game shape are different. I'm blown but don't want to admit it.

"You okay?" Prof asks when he comes in. I nod, but my heavy breathing betrays me.

"I want to stay in. I want to—"

"That's a lot of *I*'s coming from the captain. Best for the team," he reminds me. I nod then point at the bench, letting Coach know I need a rest. We run another play, a give-and-go that gets me another assist and Prof his first points of the game. Fresh comes in for me at the buzzer.

"You know the game plan, stick to it." I smack my wide chest against Fresh's skinny one.

"I don't want to mess up and be a failure," Fresh whispers. "What if I do the wrong—"

"You might fail, but that doesn't mean you are a failure, so play hard, smart, strong."

Fresh doesn't score but plays good D and makes no fouls. "Thanks, Randy," he says with a smile as I take his place on the court, but stops smiling when I point proudly at the C on my uniform. "I mean, Captain."

"So, an undefeated season?" Nick Barton, the reporter for Al.com, asks me, Show, and Coach. It's not really a question, but then again, how would I know? Language Arts was never my best subject. Now, thanks to the amazing Mr. Smith's thumb drive, every subject is my best subject.

"We have some great players, but I owe a lot of this to our captain, Randy Sullivan," Show says. I wonder if Coach made him say those words, because I know he doesn't believe them.

"But going forward, you're down a big piece with Dallas Rogers out," the reporter guy says.

"True, Dallas put up a lot of points," Coach starts. "But I think our captain can make up in leadership what he lacks in scoring skills. Besides, the point guard makes other players better. It's an unselfish position. It is exactly the kind of position you want for your team captain."

Coach and Show go on some more, but I don't say a word, playing the strong, silent type.

"So, Randy, do you have anything to say?" Nick Barton asks me directly.

I remember when Mr. Robinson asked me that and I didn't answer. Where did that get me? Here. I also remember when the woman from Child Protective Services asked me that after Aunt Angie snitched out the conditions Mom and I were living in. I told her the truth and where did that get me? Living with my aunt and visiting my mom in the hospital, when she's not on suicide watch. If I've learned anything this school year it's that doing the right thing means nothing.

"Randy, anything to say?" Nick Barton asks again.

"I do my only talking to my team before the game, and then I let my actions do the talking on the court," I say. Coach beams with pride. "We can talk after we win the state championship!"

I offer high fives to my coach and to Show, but not to the reporter. Instead my hand accepts the business card with contact info. He takes photos of the three of us. I hope Yo doesn't have his phone in the hospital, because I know it's going to crush him not getting his picture in the paper.

"Wait a second, Randy," Coach says after the rest of the team has piled out of Coach's and Show's dad's big vans. It was my idea to bring the team to visit Yo. I doubt all of us will be allowed to visit Yo at the same time, but it seems following the rules isn't something that interests me much anymore.

"What is it, Coach?" I ask.

"I want to thank you for showing such strong leadership on and off the court," he says. I try to thank him, but he talks right over me. "I need you to do something else for me. Can you?"

I look out the window at the UAB hospital. Yo's on four, Mom's on seven. I'm lost in thought. "Randy, if I ask you something, you need to answer. And if the answer is ever no, then I need to find myself a new captain, even in the playoffs."

"I understand."

"Some teachers are asking me about the sudden improvement in the team's grades." He talks slowly like he thinks I'm stupid. "Miss Torrez noticed that no one is showing up for the tutoring sessions, so you need to get the team to attend."

I nod.

"While Dallas might not come back from this injury, it is vital that everyone stays eligible for the playoffs, but also that everyone has good enough grades to keep or get college scholarships."

"I understand," I repeat. I also understand that college for me is a fantasy but not my future.

"Eddie, Reggie, and Dallas—that's the only way they'll make it out of Birmingham."

I just keep nodding and muttering yes.

"If something happens to the tutoring program, they won't make it." Coach points a finger at me, waving it in my face. "You don't want to let your teammates down, do you?"

I'm scared to answer no, but I do. Coach trades the waving finger for a thumbs-up.

I let everybody else wish Yo well, while I hang
in the back. All the guys are laughing except
one. Yo. His mouth is open and laughter is
coming out, but it's not real. The more I think
about Coach, Mr. Smith, and what I've done,
that doesn't seem real either.

"We need to get back," Coach says, taking
charge since I'm lost in thought again.

"Go ahead without me," I say, not following
him for once. "I'll catch the bus."

After everybody's out of the room, I pull
up a chair and sit by Yo's bed. I can tell he's
exhausted from having to put on the happy act.
He'll sleep away the day like Mom used to do.

I know better but ask out of habit. "How're you feeling?"

He pushes the button for the bed to recline. "I didn't just rip my ACL, Randy," he says to the ceiling. "I broke my life."

"Your knee will get better."

"And my life?" Yo tries to pull me into a swirling swill of negativity. "It is over. No college is going sign somebody with a bum knee, a bad attitude, and an empty head."

"I thought you got all A's!" I joke but he doesn't laugh. Instead he moans in pain.

"If I don't have basketball, then I have nothing to live for. If I can't—"

"It's a tough break. But you will get back to the court again."

But Yo's not having it. His setback has already snowballed into a catastrophic event in his head. He rails against Coach and Mr. Smith, but mostly himself. "This is my fault. I got hurt. I cheated. I was—"

"There's no 'I' in the word *team*." It's a cliché, but I dunk it.

Another moan. "Last year, when I wouldn't

cheat and tried to do it right, I got frozen out. It was like I never existed. Now that I'm hurt, same thing. It is like I'm already dead. A ghost."

"Look, when you get back to school it won't be that way. Come to tutoring and practice."

I try cheering him up, but he's not having it. I'd invite Connie to help, but I know that's not a good idea. I wonder if this is the "boring" Yo, who Connie mentioned but I rarely saw.

"If I can't play ball again, I don't know what I'll do." Yo continues riding the downhill-thought express train. "No sense to stay in school. No sense in doing anything. I might as—"

And I've heard enough. "Yo, stop talking like this. It is not the end of the world."

"You better leave," Yo snaps. "Surprised you didn't follow Coach out the door. You do whatever he asks you to do. You're not a captain, Randy. You're slave with a C on your shirt."

I stand and kick the chair. "Take that back." Yo puts his arms over his eyes except there's no light to block, just my raging face, the skin maybe as red as my hair. "Take that—"

"You don't know anything about it." Yo's voice drops like it hurts to speak.

"About what?"

"About what it's like to feel this way half the time," Yo says. "And the other half, to feel like you're on top of the world. I am so tired. I just want to sleep and not wake up."

I bend over the bed and grab Yo's arms, ripping them away from his face. I can see even in the darkness that his eyes are red from crying. I pull his arm to his side and then press my hands against his strong biceps. He tries to get free, but fails. "Don't you *ever* say that again."

"You're not my captain. You're a cheater and a follower. I don't listen to you," Yo says.

"I'm sorry, Dallas," I whisper. "But I do know exactly what you're going through."

"How?"

I pick up the chair and move close to the bed, like Mom used to do when she was telling me stories. This time I tell Yo stories about my mom, from her first suicide try when I was four to the last one just a few weeks ago.

The first two tournament victories are blowouts. We're a stronger team with me on point rather than Yo, since all I do is pass to Show and Reg. That will change in the semi-final against Lee. I plan to drive the lane hard to knock down 47 and turn him into my own personal whack-a-mole.

I kept my word to Coach and got team members to show up for a fake tutoring session. Mr. Smith hands out a thumb drive with the next week's assignments while I stand by the door. Just like on the court, I'm on point and on guard for any unfamiliar face who wants to spy.

Connie joins me at the door. She slips the thumb drive deep into my pocket. "Good luck tonight, my captain." I don't know how she makes the word "captain" sound so hot, but she does.

"Thanks, but we're not going to need it. We're going to own those guys. We're—"

I stop when there's a knock at the door. As planned, every head in the room starts to examine the worksheets Mr. Smith had put on their desks. I open the door and peek outside. Yo.

"Sorry, I'm late, but—"

"You invited *him*?" Connie asks me. Her juicy top lip curls into an ugly sneer.

"Coach told me to invite everybody who's been tutoring with Mr. Smith, so—"

"He's not on the team," she whispers. I can see from the look on Yo's face that he heard her anyway.

"What's going on, Mr. Sullivan?" Mr. Smith asks as he walks toward the door.

"He needs our help. It's not fair." I reflect on Yo lecturing me about unfairness by telling me about the story of his hard life, moving around with parents who didn't act like parents.

Mr. Smith opens the door. He examines Yo: crutches under his arms, frown on his face, outside looking in.

"Dallas, you need to leave." Smith sounds like a computerized voice. "This is for—"

"No, he needs our help." I brace myself as if Smith was a guard breaking toward the net.

"*No* is a word, Mr. Sullivan, that I understand does not belong on your vocabulary list."

Connie tugs on my arm and guides it to the door. Together we shut it in Yo's face.

"What should we do, Randy?" Show asks, the first time he's asked my opinion since his head swelled three times its normal size. Carver is killing us. I have no problem getting the ball deep to the big men, but Carver's D bounces on the ball holder quicker than vultures on roadkill. Our team keeps taking bad shots or pushing the ball back out to the point. Hitting jumpers isn't the captain's role.

I glance at the clock. Two minutes left, ten points down. I'm out of patience—and clichés.

Coach starts diagramming a play as if he can figure out a double-digit move. I glance at the stands, finding almost no familiar

faces, no Angie (working) and no Yo (just
sulking, I hope).

Connie and her crew try to breathe life
into us, and as much as I love her mouth-to-
mouth, the heart of this team is gone. Me.
Listening to Yo's busted dreams and brutal
accusations took the air out of me. I'm pushing
the ball up the court, not passing. I'm playing
but not a player.

Coach shouts instructions but I tune
him out, like I should have been doing from
day one. All that stuff about integrity and
intelligence. As his voice grows louder and
the clock ticks down, I know there's only one
thing he's ever cared about, and it's not me. It
is winning so he can keep his job.

And guess what? I bought it. But I was
wrong to think there was a no-return policy
on that decision. I wipe the sweat off my brow,
and it almost feels cleansing. I can't wait for the
shower. In fact, I don't.

"Coach, I quit," I say with two minutes left.
I wish I had the captain's handbook to shred
and pour over him like the confetti I imagined

would come with a state championship. "Fresh, you're in."

Fresh looks at Coach and then back at me. Coach nods at him. "Go get 'em, Fresh," I say.

"Thanks, Cap," Fresh says, which helps block out the angry words Coach yells at my back.

I head toward the locker, saying over my shoulder, "I'm not the captain of anything."

"Yo, are you in there?" I pound on the door
of his apartment. All the lights are off. I
hear a noise, but the lights don't go on. It's
Wednesday, so his grandma's at church, but Yo
never goes anymore.

I pound the door harder, but still nothing.

I heard his words the other day, but more
than that, I heard what he didn't say and the
tone of his voice—the voice of someone who
has lost everything and therefore has nothing
left to lose. Mom taught me that you can't
bargain with someone who has no chips to put
on the table.

"Yo! Yo!" I'm yelling even louder than

Coach did when I turned my back on his team. It was never my team. That was just something he said to make me do things his way.

I pull out my phone and use the flashlight app to peer through the window into the dark apartment, but there's nothing to see but more darkness. My finger twitches as it nears the too-familiar numbers on the keypad—9-1-1— for what I fear is a too-familiar scene.

If I'm wrong, nothing is lost. If I'm right, everything is saved. Once again, I'm caught between two choices that seem so clear until you get right on top of them; then it's a blur.

My phone buzzes. A text from Connie— just a few angry words, but enough to tell me that she heard whose side I chose at the game. My heart breaks, but just briefly.

I shatter the window glass on Yo's apartment door. No alarm goes off. I turn the dead bolt and go inside. I switch on the light. Yo sits in a chair, his hands covering his face, a brace supporting his knee, and a rifle sitting at his feet. "It's okay, Yo," I reassure him.

Yo tries speaking, but the weight of words

is too much for someone so broken. I call for help and sit with him, back in the darkness, saying nothing but sharing everything. The EMTs arrive quickly and check him out. "He needs a 72-hour hold," I tell them in a take-charge voice.

I pick up Yo's cell. "I'll call his mother and let her know what's going on."

"Who are you?" the younger of the EMTs asks me.

"I'm his friend," I say. And I was finally the leader I needed to be. I was on point.

With my season over, I have enough focus and
energy to visit Mom again. I call every day
until she sends word that she'll see me. I dress
up like it's a school dance, not that I've ever
been to one. The security check seems to last
longer than before. I think there's some sort
of formula about proportion between how bad
you want something and how long it takes to
get it.

Mom and I start with the usual song and
dance about me wanting her to come home,
and her saying she doesn't trust herself to be at
home. Mom's big about trusting the process,
while I've learned not to trust the process or

the system. I can trust only myself to do the right thing.

Then I tell her about Mr. Smith, Coach, and finally about Yo. Her green eyes shine for the first time when I mention that I'm going to tell the truth about the lie.

"If I don't, then it's on me if the same thing happens next year," I say, determined.

"So I guess you're still captain. You're still standing up for what is really best for the team, not in the short term but in the long term. You're seeing the big picture."

I brush aside a blush. "I got lost trying to figure out what mattered, what—"

"What you valued," she finishes my sentence like only a true mother knows how.

"That's why you're here, Mom. It's not to protect me. It is to get healthy because—"

She turns her hands over so we're palm to palm. "I'm doing what is best for our team, not in the short term, but in the long term. Randy, you'll always be the captain of our team."

"I think that's what I valued most. Being captain and what it meant." I recite the qualities of a good captain. I know it by heart from the *Team Captain Handbook*. "And of all those things, integrity is what matters most."

"I am so proud of you." She almost smiles, but I get a real smile when I tell her what I'll do after I leave her. She hugs me and invites me to visit her again. That's her values in action.

Outside the hospital is a mailbox. I drop an envelope with a thumb drive and a note explaining the cheating program. The envelope is addressed to Nick Burton, the Al.com reporter.

ABOUT THE AUTHOR

Patrick Jones is a former librarian for teenagers. He received lifetime achievement awards from the American Library Association and the Catholic Library Association in 2006. Jones has authored several titles for the following Darby Creek series: Turbocharged (2013); Opportunity (2013); The Dojo (2013), which won the YALSA Quick Picks for Reluctant Young Adult Readers award; The Red Zone (2014); The Alternative (2014); Bareknuckle (2014); and Locked Out (2015). He also authored *The Main Event: The Moves and Muscle of Pro Wrestling* (2013), which received the Chicago Public Library's Best of the Best Books list. While Patrick lives in Minneapolis, he still considers Flint, Michigan, his home. He can be found on the web at www.connectingya.com.